Mittens at School

story by **Lola M. Schaefer**
pictures by **Susan Kathleen Hartung**

HARPER
An Imprint of HarperCollinsPublishers

For Rogan
—L.M.S.

For Phoebe
—S.K.H.

I Can Read Book® is a trademark of HarperCollins Publishers.

Library of Congress Cataloging-in-Publication Data is available.
ISBN 978-0-06-170224-2 (trade bdg.) — ISBN 978-0-06-170223-5 (pbk.)

12 13 14 15 16   SCP   10 9 8 7 6 5 4 3 2 1   ❖   First Edition

Mittens is at school.

He will be Nick's show-and-tell.

"Sit here, Mittens," says Nick.

"Show-and-tell will be later."

Mittens watches Nick write.

Mittens watches Nick paint.

Mittens wants something to do.

"It's time for gym class,"
says Nick. "Wait here, Mittens.
We will be back soon."
Mittens sits and waits.

But he wants something to do.

Mittens runs to the math table.

Clink. Clink. Clink.

He pushes the counting beads.

CRASH!

The beads crash to the floor.

Mittens jumps down.

What can he do now?

Mittens runs to the piano.

Plink. Plink. Plink.

He walks across the keys.

SLAM!

The piano lid slams shut.

Mittens jumps down.

What can he do now?

Mittens runs to the bookcase.

He jumps up.

Flip. Flip. Flip.

He flips the pages of a book.

The class comes back.

BAM!

The book falls.

"Who dropped that book?"
asks the teacher.

Slowly, Mittens steps out.
"Meow."

"Who are you?"
asks the teacher.

"This is Mittens," says Nick.
"He's my show-and-tell."

"Hello, Mittens,"
says the teacher.
"Come meet our class."

At last,
Mittens has something to do!

Mittens is a good show-and-tell.

Purr. Purr.